DAWN OF THE KAIJU
ERIC S BROWN

SEVERED PRESS
Hobart Tasmania

DAWN OF THE KAIJU

DAWN OF THE KAIJU

Specialist Kerry doubted he would make it out of the cave alive. That sure didn't stop him from trying though. Sweat slicked his skin and his breath came in ragged gasps. He could hear the cries and shrieks of the creatures behind him as he ran. Kerry knew it was stupid, but he risked a glance over his shoulder anyway. His heart froze in his chest as he met the gaze of a Kaiju. It came racing along the cave's ceiling towards him. The sparks that flew every time the thing yanked its claws free of the cave and plunged them in again, pulling itself forward as fast as he could run, matched the glow of its blazing yellow eyes. The chainmail-like scales that covered the Kaiju's body shimmered as they reflected the light given off by the small lamp attached to the front of his combat helmet. The white knuckled grip with which he clutched the automatic shotgun he carried grew even tighter.

No one had suspected that there might be Kaiju still alive within the cave when his squad had been sent in. According to all the data that the eggheads had, the Kaiju were supposedly a thing of the past, extinct and forgotten by the world of man outside of legends and Japanese cartoons.

The plan had been simple. Go in, find a fossilized Kaiju corpse, extract DNA material from if possible, and bring it topside to be shipped off for study.

The caves of mount Jien were the center of numerous Kaiju legends dating back to before the birth of civilization in the Eastern world. If Kerry remembered what he told at the pre-op briefing correctly, Dr. Johnson had selected Mount Jien because of those legends and it seemed as good a place as any place to begin the United States search for the creatures. Dr. Johnson and his supporters among the powers that be wanted to use the genetic material they hoped to find there, not only to prove the existence of Kaiju, but also to bring the creatures back in the modern world as weaponized instruments of destruction.

Kerry had been forced to sign a stack of non-disclosure papers regarding the security of the project. He had ran "black ops" before but never anything like this one. Despite the project's level of secrecy, the whole thing sounded like a cakewalk to him at the time. Had he known then what he knew now, he would have never signed on.

Seeing rays of sunlight piercing the darkness of the cave up ahead of him, Kerry poured on the speed with everything his body had left to give. Beta squad was waiting outside the cave with two evac birds ready to fly out the genetic material the moment it was delivered to them. Every attempt Kerry had made at reaching them over the comm link inside his helmet had failed. The rock of the cave itself combined with the low-level radiation that permeated Mount Jien had caused a lot of interference with the squads' comms as he and Alpha squad had descended into the mountain. In the last quarter of an hour, that interference had grown worse, cutting off his link to the topside team entirely.

Kerry sprinted through the mouth of the cave, emerging into a clearing that separated the bottom of Mount Jien from the jungle surrounding it. The full strength of the midday sun stung his eyes. They blinked rapidly trying to adjust to it.

"Incoming!" he screamed at the top of his lungs. He whirled around, hoping Beta squad had his back, to face the Kaiju scrambling along the roof of the cave towards him. Jerking up his weapon, he let loose, firing a three round burst at the Kaiju. The first round struck just in front of the Kaiju's position, whining, as it ricocheted off rock. His second and third rounds found their target. The Kaiju cried out as its left arm was blown clean away from where it connected to the thing's shoulder and the Kaiju dropped with a loud thud to the cave floor. The creature's orange blood glowed where it splashed in the shadows of the cave. Scurrying to its feet, the Kaiju flashed rows of gleaming metal like teeth at him, before it sprang forward once more.

The Kaiju raised its remaining arm to take a swipe at Kerry with the long claws that tipped the ends of its fingers. Kerry met it with another three round burst at near point blank range. The impact of the rounds sent the Kaiju staggering backwards as they ripped its chest apart.

Inside the cave, Kerry could see the yellow glows of several more sets of Kaiju eyes racing towards him. He held down his weapon's trigger, trying to hose the creatures, but was rewarded only with the thuck-thuck-thuck sound of the automatic shotgun's hammer striking an empty chamber.

It was in that moment that Kerry realized he was making his stand against the Kaiju alone. Support fire from Beta squad had never joined his own. He spun around to scream at the Major who was the mission's CO, but the Major wasn't there or rather at least not all there. Bits and pieces of the men of Beta squad lay scattered all around the clearing. One of the mission's helicopters was gone, the other not much more than a burning pile of wreckage amid the trees. It looked as if it attempted to take off only to be brought down. Several shot up Kaiju bodies lay in the clearing as well.

Kerry's reeling mind never got the chance to process the scene before him fully. A wounded, but very much still alive Kaiju bounded on to him, taking him to the ground. He struggled against the creature as it brought its head down and its metal like teeth closed on his forehead. The last sound Kerry heard was that of his own skull crunching inward.

****

Dr. Johnson sat in front of General McCurry's desk, nervously drumming the fingers of his left hand on the arm of his chair. He had only been waiting on the General for a few minutes, but they had passed as if they were eons. When the door to the office finally opened and the General came in to take his seat across the desk from Johnson,

Johnson nearly leapt out of his chair.

"Take it easy, doctor," McCurry ordered him. "It's not as if I am going to have you taken outside and shot, though there are certainly those above me who would approve of such action considering how things are playing out."

"Thank you, General," Johnson managed weakly, after clearing his throat.

"Have you had a chance to see the news today?" McCurry asked.

Johnson shook his head.

"Japan is a war zone. Their entire military structure has been mobilized and put into action. Even so, they're losing ground every hour. Most of their cities are nothing more than rubble now and refugees are fleeing the country by the boatloads."

Johnson stared at McCurry not sure how to respond.

McCurry opened a folder he had carried into the office with him and handed a photo from it to Johnson who accepted it with trembling a hand.

"That's a satellite shot of Mount Jien from half an hour an ago," McCurry told him.

"God in heaven, help us," Johnson muttered as he looked at the photo. The words "ant hill" was a good way of describing what Mount Jien had become. Thousands of small Kaiju forms moved over the mountain and around its base. They looked to be tearing the mountain apart.

"Just what are those creatures doing, doctor?" McCurry asked, "And more importantly, just how many of them are there?"

Johnson swallowed hard, still staring at the photo. "They... they appear to be taking the mountain apart, General," Johnson answered. "And as to your other question, I honestly have no idea. We didn't expect to find any living Kaiju inside the mountain, General, and you know that."

"You're going to have to do better than that, Dr. Johnson. Japan is one of our allies and we have just unleashed Hell on Earth upon them."

General McCurry took the photo back and placed it on top of his desk where they both could see it. "I'll ask again, doctor, why are they taking the mountain apart?"

"Best guess?" Dr. Johnson croaked.

McCurry nodded.

"There's a Mother Kaiju below it and the creatures are trying to free it."

"Wanna explain to me what a Mother Kaiju is?"

"It's a term those of us in the field use to refer to a giant Kaiju. Take one of the Kaijus you see in that photo and imagine it standing hundreds of feet tall, with the same claws, scales, and speed."

McCurry's eyes bugged out for a moment, but he recovered his composure quickly. "Let me get this straight. You're telling me something like one of those giants from all those old school Japanese monster movies might be real and those little devils are trying to release it?"

"Yes, General McCurry, I am afraid I am."

"And this Mother Kaiju is going to go on a rampage like all the little ones when it gets free?"

"You can count on that, General," Johnson nodded. "I've never encountered a Kaiju legend or myth where the creatures were anything less than full out engines of destruction."

"The Japanese government and our own are considering nuking Mount Jien as we speak. Would that be an effective means of stopping them, Dr. Johnson?"

Johnson shrugged. "No one studying Kaiju alive today has ever encountered a living one before, so I can't say with any real certainty. Mount Jien itself is the source of a very peculiar radiation, so I doubt any radioactivity from the means you suggest dealing with the things would affect them. That said, the initial blast of the exploding bomb or bombs would. The blast would slay those on the surface, but none that remained underground and worse, using such a bomb might help release any Mother Kaiju trapped below the mountain itself."

McCurry grunted. "Though Mount Jien remains the center of their activity, for now, there are other places in Japan the smaller Kaiju appear to be digging as well and a good number of the things have simply vanished into the ocean."

Dr. Johnson found himself on the edge of tears as he spoke. "There are those who believe the Kaiju once ruled the Earth, General, and that a climate change, much like one that made the dinosaurs extinct, wiped them out. What we're seeing now though indicates the Kaiju didn't die off, General. They merely went dormant underground and beneath the oceans. The small Kaiju will sweep across the globe like locusts, destroying everything in their path, as they search for more of their kind to be awakened."

"Just how many of these creatures are you saying there are, Dr. Johnson?"

"Again, General, I can't even begin to guess, but I would wager far too many," Johnson slumped in his chair. "It appears the Kaiju Apocalypse has begun and I am responsible for it."

****

The Bushido's heavy tracks crunched over the rubble filling the street as the tank rolled backwards in retreat. Commander Yen stood in its cupola blazing away at the advancing horde of Kaiju closing in on it. The anti-personnel machine gun rounds tore a dozen or more of the creatures to shreds as spent shell casing clanged from the chattering weapons to bounce onto the tank's armored top.

Its main gun thundered, sending a shell into the center of the Kaiju mass. The proximity of the explosion shook Mien in the driver compartment of the tank.

"That was the last one!" Kota reported over the comlink shared by the three members of the Bushido's crew. "The main gun is out!"

All three had seen the rest of their unit decimated by the Kaiju. Though at most, each Kaiju stood only two feet taller than a full sized man did, the creatures were much stronger. Their clawed hands were capable of opening a tank up if enough of the things worked together to do so.

The same scene had unfolded time and time

again across the length of Japan. Everywhere the army chose to make a stand, they were slaughtered. While the Japanese military held a technological edge over the Kaiju, there were just too many of the monsters.

Commander Yen longed for air support, but he knew none would be coming. The great, desperate hope had been that the air force could turn the tide and send the Kaiju burrowing their way back into the earth from which they had come. That hope proved to be a forlorn one though.

One out of every hundred or so Kaiju sprouted wings. These new monsters took to the sky to confront the planes and helicopters that rained death upon their brothers. Their small size and maneuverability made them difficult targets to engage directly for the planes and easily over matched any helicopters the Japanese sent against them.

"Get us out of here!" Commander Yen ordered.

"Giving her everything she's got and then some, sir!" Mien shouted.

The Bushido came about in the street, turning its rear to the Kaiju, as Yen ducked back inside the vehicle and slammed its top hatch shut above him.

Clearing the rubble, the Bushido roared forward at its top speed. It wasn't fast enough.

The Kaiju came swarming over the tank. Yen heard one of the things straining to open the hatch above him. Other Kaiju ripped away at the tank's armor on all its side with their claws. Still more combined their efforts to snap free the tracks of its left side. The Bushido lurched to a halt as they did so.

"Mien!" Commander Yen shouted in warning.

"She's dead, sir!" Mien answered. "We aren't going anywhere without repairs!"

Kota was in a panic. "What do we do?"

Commander Yen drew the pistol holstered on his belt. "We die with honor!" he roared before the hatch above him was yanked free and thrown aside. Two scale covered hands plunged into the Bushido to grab hold of him. Their claws sunk into his flesh like meat hooks, dragging him upwards and out of the tank. To his credit, Yen was able to get off a shot at the Kaiju holding him before the hands of a second Kaiju closed around his head and took it from his shoulders in an explosion of blood.

Mien drew his own sidearm as Commander Yen vanished from sight and Kota snatched up the machine gun he kept in his section of the tank. Both of them managed to fire on the first Kaiju that slid inside the tank with them. Kota screamed as the thing's orange blood splattered onto his arms and face. It sizzled on his skin, burning like acid, all the way to the bone.

The Kaiju's bullet ridden corpse flopped to one side as another stuck its head down into the tank. It flashed rows of razor teeth at Mien in a feral snarl.

Mien hurriedly turned his pistol, shoving its barrel into his mouth, and he squeezed its trigger.

****

General McCurry sat at the head of the table in the Pentagon's war room. The room was filled with the head officers of each of the United States' military branches as well as Dr. Johnson and several other key scientists at work on understanding the Kaiju well enough to better engage them.

"Japan has fallen," McCurry informed those gathered. A hush fell over the room as everyone's attention centered on him.

"China and Russia are under siege," he went on. "Australia is holding on by a thread."

"What about Europe?" Someone asked.

"Most of Europe has gone silent," McCurry frowned.

"So it's true then?" Dr. Johnson asked. "The Mother Kaiju have awakened."

McCurry nodded. "Yes, we have confirmed reports of three separate Mother Kaiju. Two in what's left of Japan and a third somewhere off the coast of Australia. Though there haven't been any major Kaiju incursions onto U.S. soil as yet, you can rest assured they are coming."

Calling up a holographic globe in the center of the table, McCurry pointed at several regions of the Pacific and Atlantic oceans. "American naval forces have already engaged the Kaiju along the Atlantic seaboard and off the coast of Hawaii."

"Are we going to try to defend Hawaii?" an admiral smoking a cigar in the rear of the room asked.

McCurry shook his head sadly. "We can't. We don't have the resources for it. Everything we have is being deployed along the mainland's borders in hopes of stopping the Kaiju before they truly enter the U.S. We're also evacuating all the civilian population that we can inland. I don't have to tell you that it's not going well either. People are scared. To them, this looks like the end of the world and at this point, I can't say it's not."

"Do we have a plan, General McCurry?" another officer asked.

"Beyond digging in and trying to hold our ground, no, we don't. We do have advantages that places like Japan didn't though. We are aware that the Kaiju have fliers among their ranks and we are now able to put the total known number of smaller Kaiju at five million, give or take a few ten thousand."

"Five million?" someone muttered.

"On the upside," McCurry quickly added, "The Kaiju's numbers have stopped growing exponentially as they were at the start of all this madness. They appeared to have leveled off. No matter how large a threat the smaller Kaiju are, the Mother Kaiju should be our primary concern. I am correct in that aren't I, Dr. Johnson?"

Johnson tried to melt into his chair as the room's attention turned to him.

"Dr. Johnson?" McCurry asked again.

"Uh, yes. . ." Johnson answered at last. "That would be the case. The smaller Kaiju can't breed. It's the Mother Kaiju, the large ones, that spawn new Kaiju. Thanks to footage we were sent from Japan before the entire country went dark, we've been able to confirm our theory on that."

"Just how fast can they breed, Dr. Johnson?"

"A single Mother Kaiju can spawn up to two hundred of the lesser ones within the space of an hour once it enters its gestational period. It looks something like that scene from Gremlins when Spike gets wet and they just shoot off his body inside of eggs."

"What about the Mother Kaiju themselves, doctor? How do they reproduce and how quickly?"

"We don't have *any* data on that yet, General, but all of us working on it agree that it must be a much slower process," Johnson answered, using his pointer finger to push his glasses upwards on his nose. "As thus, it would be to our great advantage to make eliminating the Mother Kaiju we know are out there our priority as quickly as possible."

"The fliers were a surprise that the Japs weren't counting on," McCurry pointed out. "Do you think there are still other types of lesser Kaiju we haven't seen yet, Dr. Johnson?"

Johnson shrugged. "Only God knows that for sure, General, but I wouldn't rule it out."

****

Captain Gary Peart watched the battle that was taking place on the surface via the large screen that covered the forward section of the Compton's bridge. The Compton wasn't officially part of the battle group that engaged the Kaiju off the coast of North Carolina. She had been on patrol in the region long before the battle group had arrived and her orders hadn't changed overly much.

Peart sat in his command chair, the decision of whether or not to go to the battle group's aid weighing heavily upon him. The Compton was the first sub of her class and her tech made that of most of the US fleet's seem long outdated in comparison. The patrol to which she was currently assigned had been meant to be a shakedown cruise of sorts for her. He didn't question that the Compton could more than handle herself in the conflict and her updated orders now included making every possible effort to prevent any Kaiju she encountered from making landfall on US soil. Still, the battle group in the distance was being slaughtered. It consisted of two destroyers and a single battleship, the Roosevelt.

One of the destroyers was already damaged to the point of sinking. The destroyer was dead in the water. Its hull was breached by a single swipe of the Mother Kaiju's hand that it was engaged with. Sailors in lifeboats were pouring off it in what looked to be a vain attempt at survival. The Roosevelt and the other destroyer were emptying everything they had at their disposal into the Mother Kaiju. Tracer rounds from their deck mounted gun emplacements streaked through the darkness of the night towards the giant monster. The Mother Kaiju stood several hundred feet tall, the upper portion of its body above the ocean's surface. Peart watched as it closed in on the remaining functional destroyer even as the Roosevelt's main cannons thundered. A fiery explosion blossomed on the Mother Kaiju's right shoulder causing the creature to lumber sideways. The Mother Kaiju stayed on its feet though, quickly recovering from the impact. It reached the destroyer, with clawed hands lashing out to grab hold of the destroyer's forward deck and plunge that end of the ship beneath the waves.

Peart hadn't heard of any Mother Kaiju this close to the United States. There certainly hadn't been mention of one in the last batch of reports he'd received. He was on the verge of ordering his crew to take the giant monster with the Compton's guns when his XO, Olsen, shouted at him.

"Sir! We've got incoming. CBDR."

Peart's head jerked around to look at his XO. Though Olsen kept an air of professional composure, Peart knew the man well enough to know that the Compton was in trouble.

"Another one of those?" Peart asked, gesturing at the image of the Mother Kaiju on the forward screen.

Olson shook his head. "No sir. I believe it's a swarm of lesser Kaiju!"

Peart's own heart leapt into his throat. For a sub like the Compton, facing a swarm was far worse than going head to head with one of the Mothers. For all her upgrades to her tech, the Compton only possessed two weapon systems she could bring to bear on her enemies. Those were the traditional stern and aft torpedo launchers and the long range nukes she carried. Her sides were as exposed as those of any other submarine. If the tactics of the Kaiju swarm were consistent with those of others he read about it, they would close on the Compton as fast as they were able and then tear her hull apart with their bare hands from the outside as she sat helpless against them.

"Evasive maneuvers! Engines to full military speed!" Peart ordered.

Those orders given, he asked, "Time to contact?"

"The swarm is moving at 25 knots, sir. Even with our engines at full, they'll overtake in less than three minutes!"

"Take the swarm with our aft launchers!" Peart said, "Fire at will! Maximum spread!"

"Target locked!" The guns station informed him, then added, "Batteries released!"

The view on the forward screen changed to show an image of the swarm in pursuit of the Compton. Peart winced as he saw the swarm. Even with the screen set to a wide-angle image, the swarm took up the whole screen, filling it was a mass of gray scaled creatures.

"Contact!" The gunnery officer yelled a fraction of a second before the screen lit up as a series of explosions ripped their way across the forward ranks of the Kaiju.

Peart couldn't guess at how many Kaiju died in the blasts, but he knew it wasn't enough. The cloud of gray merely shifted as it continued forward, more Kaiju surging onward to take the place of those that had perished.

Tapping open a channel to the Compton's engine room, Peart screamed over it, "I need more power to the engines! Now!"

He knew it was already too late though, even as

the words left his mouth. He heard the loud clangs of the lesser Kaiju making contact with the Compton's hull.

"The Kaiju have overtaken us, sir!" Olsen shouted. "We have breaches happening all over the aft section!"

"Emergency bulkheads are dropping in place but we're still taking on water!" another officer was yelling.

The entire bridge had become a scene of chaos and panic.

"We have reports of Kaiju *inside* the Compton, sir!" Olson told him.

"Open a ship wide channel for me," Peart demanded.

"Channel open, sir!"

"All hands, this Captain Peart! Abandon ship! I repeat, abandon ship!"

"Captain!" the Compton's helmsman shouted at him, gesturing toward the forward view screen.

The image there was distorted. It was more of a smear across its bending surface than anything else.

Peart had just enough time to realize what was happening before the screen shattered and a Kaiju came tearing through the forward hull. An explosion of ocean water came flooding onto the bridge in the creature's wake. The rush of water hit Peart like a runaway eighteen wheeler, trapping him in his command chair. He opened his mouth to scream and the water rushed inside him as well, filling up his lungs. Then his world became only a cold, wet blackness.

****

"Bam! Bam! Bam!" Danny squealed, ramming one of his toy robots into an equally sized, plastic T-Rex. His blue eyes were wide with excitement and glee despite the atmosphere of worry and fear around him.

Mark sat a few feet from where his son played in the grass. The rays of the early morning sun were warm as it rose above the mountains. Scott sat next to Mark, taking a swig from his already half empty bottle of beer. A cooler, mostly full of melted ice, rested at Scott's feet.

"I can't believe it," Scott was saying, though Mark was barely listening. "I mean I know things are getting bad out there but this ridiculous."

Scott must have noticed he wasn't paying attention because he reached down and splashed some of the chilled water in the cooler at Mark. Mark flinched when the cold liquid struck his sandal clad feet.

"Hey!" Mark exclaimed.

"Got your attention, didn't it?" Scott grinned. "You zoned out on me again."

"Sorry," Mark shrugged.

"It's okay. I get it," Scott said, gesturing at Danny. "You've got a lot more to think about than me when push comes to shove."

Danny was still playing away in front of them. The robot toys appeared to be winning and driving the dinosaur ones back in retreat.

"I guess I do at that," Mark admitted.

"If we're not safe this far inland, the way I figure

it, we're not safe anywhere," Scott said, finishing his beer.

"I know," Mark nodded. "It's just, we didn't hardly have time to grab anything before those army guys..."

"National Guard," Scott corrected him.

"Whatever. Before they grabbed us and brought us here."

"Best be glad they did, son," Scott assured him. "From what I hear, they are making some kind of big stand on the coast. You and your boy are a lot better here than you would be there when the shells start flying."

Scott leaned over fishing the last two beers out of his cooler and handed one of them to Mark. Mark accepted it reluctantly. He wasn't keen on drinking in front of Danny.

Mark, not wanting to be rude, opened it, as he looked past Danny at the sea of tents and mobile homes surrounding them. The area that had once been a wide-open field was now a refugee camp that sprawled all the way across the valley. It didn't have a proper name that Mark knew of, but Scott liked to call it Camp Screwed. Why, Mark couldn't say for sure. Maybe it was because everyone here was on edge, with very little in terms of the comforts of their own, now left behind in homes that none of them ever thought they would see again. Or maybe it was because if the Army failed to stop the Kaiju, the camp would be like one big buffet bar just waiting for the monsters to reach it.

By Mark's best guess, there had to be nearly ten

thousand people in the camp as of this morning and more were still being brought in. There were rumors of other camps like this one scattered all across the western part of North Carolina. He often thought of finding someone with a car and either convincing them to take him and Danny westward or just stealing it and heading out themselves. There were three key problems with that idea. For starters, this was the south. Most of the good old boys who did have some gas for the vehicles had been herded to this camp and they also had guns. Messing with an armed redneck was never a good idea under any circumstances. Two, gas, even for the camp's generators that the National Guardsmen looked after was a very rare thing. There was no way to know for sure who had any and who didn't without asking. Doing so tipped off whoever you *were* brave enough to ask to exactly what you were thinking. And three, even if he did a get a vehicle with gas, Mark had no idea where he and Danny could run to. They were recent transplants in the South and had no family remotely within easy reach. That last part made his lips dip into a frown as he thought of his sister Laura. She had been in the middle of a four year tour of duty in the Army when all this crap with the Kaiju hit the fan. He could only pray she was okay and safe somewhere herself, though he doubted it. Knowing Laura, she would be on the front line if she could.

Mark realized Danny had stopped playing. The small, blond haired boy came over to where he sat.

"Dad, I'm hungry," he pleaded looking up into

Mark's eyes.

"They'll be setting up things for breakfast in an hour or so, Danny. It won't be long. I promise."

One good thing about the camp was that the guardsmen running it *did* make sure everyone was fed. Not that the food was great. It was usually some kind of cereal or stale pastries for breakfast with no coffee, only milk and juice to drink. Thankfully, Danny seemed rather content on living on breakfasts like that day in and day out even if Mark himself wasn't.

"I can't wait that long, Dad," Danny urged him. "I'm hungry now!"

"I'm sorry, Danny..." Mark started but Scott interrupted him.

"I think I got something, son," Scott said, digging around in the pockets of his shorts without getting up. He produced a pack of half crushed cookies and handed them to Danny.

Danny took them, tearing the wrapper open, to ram several of the cookies into his mouth at once. Through the mouthful of crunching chocolate, he said, "Thank you Mr. Wiggins!"

The remainder of the cookies in hand, Danny darted back to his toys to resume his own little private war. The dinosaurs were making a comeback, it looked like.

"Good kid you got there," Scott commented.

Mark met Scott's eyes. "Thank you. I mean that."

Scott patted the roll of fat that was his belly. "I think I'll survive," he chuckled.

****

Major Laura Riddle's Apache soared over the beach, making a sweeping run, as she overlooked the sheer amount of personnel and firepower that had been gathered below her. Rows of tanks of every kind lined the beach. Scattered among their number were numerous mobile, track mounted missile launchers. Here and there were parked APCs, their .50 Caliber machine guns facing the ocean waves. Thousands of infantrymen and support troops moved through the clustered vehicles like ants as they continued to prepare for the coming battle.

Laura's Apache was far from the only one moving about above the preparations. An alarm warned her that she needed to get her head out of her butt and start paying more attention to the airspace she was flying through. A trio of fighter jets whined by to the south, headed out away from the beach. They were the third such group she had noticed flying that way in the last few minutes. She supposed that meant the Kaiju were getting closer.

The Navy had done their best and come up short. Now it was the Army and Air force's turn to take a shot at stopping the Kaiju. If the monsters weren't stopped here and now, the Kaiju would make landfall and there would be very little left to combat them as they made their way inland into America.

Her role was to provide support to the Gamma section of the combat grid. The position was composed mostly of ground based missile launchers with a few Abrams thrown into the section to provide it a backbone should the Kaiju come into direct combat range of it. Laura wasn't sure her Apache would make much of a difference if one of the Mother creatures made it ashore if the reports she had stolen a glance at during the general briefing on this ops were correct. Just one, *one,* of the giant creatures was reported to have taken out an entire naval battle group by itself and remained a threat afterward. She supposed the best she could hope for was that it would be lesser Kaiju that charged the section of the combat grid she was assigned to. Those, she would not only be safe from, but her Apache's weapons *would* cut them to shreds.

She brought her bird around to take up a stationary position above her section of the grid and pointed it toward the ocean. As she did so, she got her first real life look at a Mother Kaiju. The water of the ocean churned and parted as the monster rose above the waves. Its three yellow eyes burnt like small suns even in the midday light. The thing stood, easily, two hundred and fifty feet tall. Its lower half resembled that of a T-Rex. The Kaiju's arms were long though and eerily human-like in their appearance. They ended in three fingered, clawed hands. Her breath caught as the Mother Kaiju opened its mouth to reveal the rows of metal, razor teeth inside it. The Mother Kaiju loosed a shriek so loud that it hurt Laura's head, even inside her Apache over the sound of the bird's engines. The ears of the poor infantry groups had to be bleeding from the sheer volume of the cry.

Batteries and the main guns of tanks up and down the beach all opened fire at once. The Mother Kaiju staggered underneath the power of the barrage that struck it but it didn't fall. Instead, it stood there enduring everything that was being thrown at it though chunks of the thing's flesh were blown clean from its body.

Oh, God, help us! Laura thought as she realized what the Mother Kaiju was doing. The giant beast was using itself as a distraction to keep everyone's attention focused on it. Even as it reeled under the firepower tearing it to shreds, thousands and thousands of smaller forms were emerging from the waves to storm the beach. The distant, man-sized Kaiju looked like little dots of moving gray from where Laura hovered watching them, but there were so, so many of them.

As the tanks, missile launchers, etc. kept their fire concentrated on the Mother Kaiju, Laura watched the infantry move forward to block the lesser Kaiju. Small arms fire joined the raging cacophony of the battle.

Laura held back. Several other birds like hers had already sped forward to meet the incoming tide of lesser Kaiju. Their rockets sent pieces of Kaiju bodies and sand skyward as they struck their targets. Laura wasn't entirely sure why she was holding back. She had flown combat ops before and never been afraid. Well, not so much as to keep her from doing her job.

At last, the Mother Kaiju fell. Its torn and

battered corpse collapsed into the waves with a splash that rained ocean water over the beach near where it went down. Laura allowed herself to feel hope that they would be able to stop the Kaiju here, and hold the creatures at bay. Then the bottom of her stomach fell out as her eyes bugged and she saw two more Mother Kaiju rising not far off the coastline. The fear that rushed through her set her into motion. She kicked her Apache's engines up to combat speed and dove into a strafing run at the Kaiju closing in on the troops in her section of the grid.

Volleys of rockets left the launchers on her Apache's small wings as its main cannon chattered, hosing the Kaiju in her path. Her Apache left a trail of mangled Kaiju corpses in its wake until she flew over the coastline and there was churning, orange tinted water beneath her.

Laura brought her Apache around hard for another run. This time, she knew she would need to be careful as to not hit the troops and vehicles she had been assigned to support. Unfortunately, in her determination to hurt the lesser Kaiju as much as she could, her course had taken her too far out from the shore and too close to one of the new Mother Kaiju that was charging the beach. She never saw its massive hand lash out at her until one of its claws clipped her Apache's tail.

Suddenly, her console was blazing with warning lights and it was all she could do to keep any kind of control. Her Apache spun about wildly in the air as she fought to keep it from going into a full out spin.

"This is Tango 2!" she cried over the bird's comm system. "I'm hit and going down!"

Laura knew she had to get her bird clear of the troops and vehicles below her before she went down. The trouble was the whole beach was full of troops and vehicles for miles in every direction. She jerked her controls with all her might, bringing the Apache around again. She was losing altitude fast and didn't have much time. She managed to angle the Apache to where it should strike the beach in between the clusters of the armies defensive lines and the open water. With any luck, it would plow straight into the ranks of the lesser Kaiju making their way ashore.

Having done all she could, she rode the bird down. A sea of snarling, snouted faces stared up at her until both her and the Kaiju she plowed into were consumed in fire.

****

The Apache fell from the sky like the hammer of an angry god. Specialist Jerome Klein threw himself flat to avoid the shrapnel sent flying from its impact. He had been a part of the hurriedly withdrawing line of infantry that failed to stop the onrush of the lesser Kaiju. His M-16 had nearly been jarred from his grasp as he struck the sand and then rolled to his feet. He came up not six feet from a monster. The Kaiju roared its fury at him and bounded towards him. Klein leveled his M-16 at the creature and popped a series of three round bursts that gutted the thing. He didn't stick around to make sure he'd finished it. He whirled about and continued his headlong rush towards the already partially overrun section of the beach the remainder of his unit was running for.

Klein noticed a Kaiju ahead of him. The things were much faster than a man on foot was, when they put their minds to it. The creature was busy chasing another soldier and catching up to her quickly. In an attempt to save her and clear his own path, Klein took a wild shot at its backside, hoping he didn't hit the female soldier in the process. The Kaiju cried out as the rifle's round dug holes in the flesh of its back along the length of its spine. Klein gave a cry himself as the creature came to a stop and spun around to face him. He was moving too fast to stop himself and he had already lowered his weapon. There was no time to bring it back up. Colliding with the creature was like smashing into a brick wall. He bounced off it and landed hard on his butt in front of the Kaiju. Jerking his head to the side, he narrowly dodged a blow that would have likely taken his head from his shoulders in a spray of blood had it made contact. The Kaiju hissed and took another swing at him. This time, Klein was able to bring up his rifle. He used it to block the blow. The rifle snapped in half in his hands but it did its job in deflecting the Kaiju's claws.

Klein's sidearm cleared its holster as the Kaiju readied itself for a third swing at him. He emptied half the pistol's mag, point blank into the thing's nose and cheeks, caving in its face. Rolling out of the path of the Kaiju's falling body, he picked himself up and kept running.

His legs pumped under him as sweat glistened on his skin. Several drops of the Kaiju's blood had landed on the barrel of his pistol. The metal of the pistol smoked from where the Kaiju blood burnt into it. He flung the weapon aside not wanting to risk getting any of the acid like stuff on his skin.

Before he even realized it, he had caught up to the rest of the fleeing troops and joined their number. Nobody was so stupid as to try to stand and fight at this point. The best any of them could do was to try to escape and regroup to fight again another day.

****

General McCurry slammed his fist into the rear part of the .50 caliber gun emplacement atop the APC. Things had gone to hell and there was no hope rallying his forces any time soon, much less winning this battle. Though it pained him greatly, he had given the general retreat order only moments before. The best preliminary estimates he was given put the battle group's losses at over fifty percent. The beach, minus the continuing stream of monsters pouring onto the sand, looked something akin to what Normandy must have looked like on D-day on a much larger scale. Clouds of black smoke drifted skyward from the wreckage of still burning tanks and APCs. His plan hadn't included a properly detailed escape strategy should things go south. This battle had been do or die from its initial planning stages and McCurry along with his troops were paying the price for that.

Many of the surviving tanks closer to the ocean had no clear escape route up the beach. They were being overrun by the incoming tide of Kaiju and they were torn apart even as they tried to retreat. The two new Mother Kaiju were moving up the beach through the remains of McCurry's force, which only added to the chaos. One of the Mother Kaiju was badly wounded. It dragged one of its legs along as it lumbered forward. Wounds leaking orange blood covered most of its body, but the thing refused to fall. The other Mother Kaiju was in far better shape though it too had suffered numerous wounds during the engagement. McCurry watched as the monster picked up a tank effortlessly, and hurled it into a group of infantrymen running for their lives.

He thumped on the APC's roof. "Get us moving!"

Though he never heard the driver reply, the driver must have heard him. The APC backed up and turned itself around before its heavy wheels sent sand spraying into the air before they found traction. Then the APC rolled forward, building speed as it went.

McCurry knew his own personal evac copter was inbound. With the battle lost, he would be needed back in Washington. As the APC sped away from the beach, McCurry took one final look at the devastation the Kaiju had wrought.

****

Several hours later, exhausted and disheartened, McCurry stepped off his copter onto the White House lawn. A cluster of security personnel were waiting for him. They hurriedly rushed him inside to where the President and other members of the hastily assembled Kaiju task force leaders were.

One of the security officers handed McCurry a bottled water on his way to the war room. McCurry twisted its top open, downing half the bottle in one long chug. Not caring how he looked having just came from a battle, he poured the remainder of the bottle over his head. The cold helped him to gather his thoughts and regain his focus.

President Stewman sat at the head of a long table. The other admirals and generals who were available at the current time lined its sides as McCurry entered and took his seat at the end opposite the president.

"General McCurry," the president nodded at him in greeting.

"Sir," McCurry acknowledged as he slumped into his chair.

"It appears you were correct that the Kaiju would make their push inland via the Atlantic Coast. Am I to understand that efforts to stop them there failed?"

"Unfortunately so, Mr. President," McCurry answered.

Admiral Fiore spoke up. "Failed might be an understatement."

McCurry nodded in agreement. "It was an outright disaster. The only good thing to come of it was that we managed to eliminate one of the Mother Kaiju and wound another so severely, I doubt it will survive for very long."

McCurry had expected to see some sign of relief in the expressions of the other officers present, but there was none to be found.

"What?" McCurry asked. "Am I missing something?"

"He doesn't know?" the President asked.

"Know what?" McCurry scanned the room, searching the faces of those present for some clue of what he was missing.

"The number of known Mother Kaiju has increased significantly while you were away, General McCurry," the President frowned.

"And things get worse from there," Fiore added.

"America is now the only country, as far as our intel can discern, that remains capable of fielding any kind of significant resistant to the Kaiju." The President called up the holographic representation of a globe in the center of the table. "Most of our places are completely overrun, their military forces in shambles."

"As a last ditch effort, China resorted to tactical nukes on their own soil. Just as Dr. Johnson predicted, the fallout has had no noticeable effect on the Kaiju and the strikes themselves, like everything else that's been tried, did nothing more than force the surviving lesser Kaiju to fall back and regroup," Admiral Fiore wrung his hands where they rested on the table top before continuing. "We will *not* be making the same mistake here. The price is too high to pay for so little gained from such strikes."

"So where does that leave us?" McCurry couldn't help but ask, though technically it was his job to have that answer.

The President merely stared at McCurry.

Fiore shrugged. "We still have the forces that were deployed along the Pacific front but pulling all of them away to deal with the Kaiju incursion from the Atlantic side may prove a bad idea."

McCurry didn't even have to think about that one. "Agreed," he said quickly. "What's the current status of the Kaiju who broke through my lines?"

"The severely wounded Mother Kaiju you mentioned has stopped moving and appears to be dying not far outside the area that your forces engaged it. Two more Mother Kaiju have joined with the other survivor that is still on the move. The three of them are pushing westward at a staggering pace, destroying everything in their path. Much of North Carolina is nothing but ruins and burning rubble."

"The refugee camps!" McCurry exclaimed. "They'll be straight in the path of those monsters."

"We know," the President said. "We're doing everything we can to evacuate those poor souls even further inland. However, most of the National Guardsmen initially assigned to that task have been pulled away from it in an effort to engage and slow the Mother Kaiju down."

"With respect, Mr. President, buying time and

retreating isn't going to save us forever," McCurry's voice was cold and hard. "Eventually, we will run out of places to run."

"The survivors of your battle group are rallying in three different locations as we speak," Fiore told him, reshaping the holographic globe into a more close up representation of the East Coast. "Here, here, here." Fiore pointed to the far western portion of North Carolina, northwestern South Carolina, and West Virginia. "We need you in the field again to take command of those groups. If you can eliminate the three Mother Kaiju in North Carolina, perhaps we can drive the lesser ones back towards the ocean and set up a new defensive line somewhere not far from the coast."

McCurry rubbed at his cheeks with the fingers of his right hand stretched across the sides of his face as he thought it over. "What makes you think a second defensive line will fare any better than our first effort to stop them?"

"No one said it would general," the President shook his head, "But at this time, trying again appears to be the only option available to us. In the meantime, the air force will do what they can to make your job easier. With any luck, by the time you return to North Carolina, they will have already downed another of the Mother Kaiju."

****

Captain Marcus Clifton was in command of the wing of F-16s that flew towards the town of Sylva. Two Mother Kaiju awaited them there. The things were moving westward as fast as their giant legs would carry them but their rate of travel was slowed by the fact that the great beasts tended to stop every so often to fully unleash their rage on the stores, homes, and buildings that lined their path.

His wing men, Burton and Higgs, were survivors of the first main battle with the Kaiju too. All three of them had faced the giant monsters before at on the beaches of North Carolina. Marcus was ready as the Mother Kaiju came into view ahead of them. The two Mother Kaiju had pulled ahead of the third one that was following them. The reports claimed that the last Mother Kaiju was wounded and simply couldn't keep up with these two. Marcus was intent on making these Mothers bleed just as badly.

"We got visual, sir," Burton said over the radio, stating the obvious.

One of the two Mother Kaiju was utterly reptilian in nature. The thing looked like a T-Rex on steroids with long, human like arms that dangled at its sides as it moved. The other was unlike anything Marcus had ever seen. It had a head shaped like a ram's right down the curled horns on the sides of its skull. The thing didn't have arms so much as it had clusters of writhing tentacles that jutted out of its shoulders where its arms should have been.

Marcus powered up his F-16's weapon systems and instantly got a lock on the lizard Kaiju with his missiles. One would think that with the Mother Kaiju being so large, it would next to impossible to miss them anyway. He knew from experience that wasn't the case. The creatures were far more agile than they appeared. He had seen Mother Kaiju like them dodge incoming missiles like a lucky infantrymen might manage to get out of the way of an incoming bullet.

"Hold your fire until we get closer," Marcus ordered.

"Ah, come on, boss man," Higgs challenged him. "Have a little faith in modern technology."

"Yeah," Burton spoke up sarcastically, "because it's done wonders in winning us this war so far!"

"Can it!" Marcus barked at them. "Pick your targets and engage on my mark!"

The trio of F-16s came zooming in, dropping in altitude to engage the Mother Kaiju better, as Marcus took a breath and got ready for the crap to hit the fan.

"Fire!" he shouted.

Missiles flew like spears, howling through the air to strike the two Mother Kaiju. Both Marcus and Higgs had targeted the lizard one. Their missiles made contract with its chest and shoulders. Bright explosions of orangish flames blossomed against the creature's scaly flesh. One of the explosions sent a chunk of the thing's right shoulder spiraling away from its body.

Burton had elected to go after the ram-like Mother Kaiju. His missiles never made contact with its body though. The thing's masses of tentacles rose up, slapping the missiles out of the air like whips. Some of its tentacles were damaged in the process, but they appeared to be healing themselves at an impossible rate.

"Break formation!" Marcus yelled as the three F-16's run carried them too close to the Mother Kaiju for his liking.

The ram Mother Kaiju sprung forward, its tentacles lashing out and upwards once more. They grabbed hold of Burton's plane and jerked it apart into numerous pieces of flaming debris that spun away from where the plane's body had been in various directions.

Burton's screams began and died in less than two seconds.

"Coyote 2 is down!" Higgs was shouting but Marcus didn't have time to think about what had happened to Burton. He had his own problems. As he and Higgs had flown past the lizard Mother Kaiju, the giant monster had clipped his F-16's left wing with its claws. Dark smoke was pouring out of the wing and alarms were going off all over his console. It was taking everything he had just to keep his F-16 flying in a straight line and not going spiraling out of control to the ground below.

"Disengage! Disengage!" Marcus was screaming but Higgs appeared to be ignoring him. He looked over his shoulder to see Higgs through his canopy, falling behind him and going into a turn.

Higgs brought his F-16 around and came in at the Mother Kaiju for a second run.

Marcus was cursing like a sailor at Higgs' stupidity, but there was nothing else he could do. He had to get out of there and could only pray he found a place to set down before his own F-16 either exploded or fell apart from the damage the

Mother Kaiju had inflicted on it. He figured that if he made it back to base alive, the least he could do was put Higgs in for a commendation for bravery despite the man's blatant disregard of command structure, because deep down, he knew Higgs wouldn't be coming home with him.

****

Mark and his son Danny had moved from living in the tent that the National Guardsmen had issued them upon their arrival at the camp to staying inside Scott's RV with him. The atmosphere of fear had continued to grow in the camp with each passing day. In the beginning, the folks cooped up inside its perimeter offered at least a strained degree of politeness to one another, but no more. It had become every person, every family, for themselves. Mark thanked God that he and Danny had met Scott on their very first day there. Scott was a good two decades older than he was and a veteran to boot. Scott was accustomed to making it through rough times. In some ways, he even seemed to thrive on them from what Mark had seen of him. They brought out the best in the grizzled old veteran.

Twice, other residents of the camp had tried to break into Scott's RV. Whether they hoped that Scott had gas in its tank or were just after food, Mark didn't care. He had helped Scott keep them away from what rightly belonged to the old vet. Each time the two of them had reported the incidents to the camp's guards, but the National Guardsmen could not do much more than apologize and tell them they were doing their best to keep order. Mark understood that the Guardsmen had become outnumbered hundreds to one as the camp's population had continued to grow. If anything, the number of Guardsmen overseeing the camp had declined as they were pulled away to join the fight against the Kaiju. Still, understanding and forgiving were two very separate things.

Danny was taking the whole thing in stride. To his young mind, the nightmare that they were living was nothing more than a great adventure. When it was over, they would be able to go home. Mark knew better. They would never see home again regardless of what happened. Their home was likely nothing more than a torn apart shell. The Kaiju pressing further and further inland would have seen to that. Danny's positive attitude played a large role in keeping Mark going. And Scott did everything he could to make sure the two of them had enough to eat and a safe place to sleep.

Food and water were becoming an issue in the camp. Mark didn't know if the camp's initial supply was merely running out or if the supply lines that kept the camp cared for had been broken by the inward press of the Kaiju.

Mark could tell more and more people were thinking of fleeing the camp but few did. He, himself, had considered doing so shortly after he and Danny arrived but hadn't. The way he saw things, there was simply nowhere to run.

There were those in the camp who had brought

generators with them. The few who still had fuel left that hadn't been used up or stolen from them gleaned what news they could from their radios and satellite TVs. Scott had neither, so Mark had to keep his nose to the ground to find out what he could from others. Most stations, he heard, were nothing more than dead air or emergency broadcast system logos now. The few that remained on the air did so at sporadic instances and talked more about the nature of the Kaiju invaders than how the war against them was going. Mark took that as a very bad sign.

The camp's rumor mill claimed that the Army had made a great stand against the Kaiju on the coast of North Carolina and was crushed there. Mark was inclined to believe it with the continuing decline of things inside the camp. *Regardless,* he told himself, *today is a new day. Maybe things will get better.*

Both he and Danny had gotten up early. They had shared dry cereal with Scott for breakfast. After that, Scott had withdrawn to the rear of the RV with a novel clutched in his hands to pass the time. Danny had pitched a fit to go outside into the camp and play, but Mark had refused to let him. Instead, the two of them played chess on the folded out table of the RV's small kitchen area.

Danny was close to beating him when the camp erupted into chaos outside the RV.

Sirens blared, drowning out the rising panicked screams of those outside the RV's walls. Scott leaped to his feet, throwing his novel aside.

"What the heck?" the old veteran raged, racing

up to where Mark and Danny sat.

"Don't know," Mark answered, "but it can't be anything good."

"You got that right!" Scott spat.

"Here, help me!" Scott motioned for Mark to help him tear up a section of the RV's floor.

Mark did so. Tucked inside the flooring was a long metal box. Scott pulled it up and out of the floor to sit it between him and Mark.

Scott's fingers flipped the box open.

Mark's eyes grew wide as he saw what was inside it.

"Dang, Scott!" he shouted. "You know these are illegal in the camp, right?"

"Shut up and start loading this one," Scott ordered, shoving a pump action shotgun into Mark's hand.

Scott picked up a belt containing a holstered pistol and began to put it on. Danny watched the two of them with utter fascination.

A weapon Mark recognized as an AR-15 was also in the box. Scott snatched it up and started loading a magazine for it once he had his belt on.

"What are the National Guardsmen going to do when they find out you have all this?" Mark stammered as he continued to load the shotgun Scott had given him.

Scott outright laughed in response. "You hear those sirens, don't you?"

Mark nodded.

"Something tells me they're going to have their hands too full to notice us, Mark. Those sirens can only mean one of two things, they're getting ready to scramble us all out of here as fast as they can, likely on foot, or the camp is already under attack."

****

It had taken some time and a great deal of effort to get his forces reassembled but McCurry had managed it. Nearly everything the United States had left in terms of military power this side of the Mississippi was again under his direct command and headed towards a city once called Asheville. That was where they would meet the Mother Kaiju and the seemingly endless swarms of lesser ones that followed the giant creatures head on.

The convoy of vehicles stretched along the road. It was led by half dozen Abram tanks. A trio of APCs followed in their wake, McCurry's among them. Behind the APCs came eight troop transports carrying the infantry assigned to the task force. Three more APCs followed the transports with two more tanks bringing up the rear. McCurry hoped it would be enough to stop the Kaiju.

Four scattered combat helicopters kept pace with the convoy. Their firepower and ability to close in the Mother Kaiju were going to be sorely needed as McCurry saw things. At this point, he would order the blasted pilots to fly down the Mother Kaijus' throats if need be. The United States wasn't likely to get another organized shot at the Mother Kaiju ravaging their way deeper into the country for some time.

McCurry bounced against the .50 caliber

weapon he sat behind as his APC jerked suddenly to a halt. Cursing, he rubbed at his bruised ribs and strained to see what the hold up was up ahead.

As he watched, the lead tanks began to fan out to the east and west. Their main cannons roared, sending shells flying at some unseen enemy beyond McCurry's field of vision. The convoy's com-net was in utter chaos. McCurry cut into it, taking over the net.

"Report!" he shouted.

"Armadillo 1 here, sir! We've encountered Kaiju and moved to engage."

McCurry felt a burning rage growing inside him. This was *his* command, blast it. He started to order the tanks back into formation, figuring the convoy could plow its way through any Kaiju ahead of it, but never got the chance. The voices of thousands of Kaiju arose from all around in a deafening chorus of shrieks and hisses.

The Kaiju came from everywhere at once, surrounding the convoy. The creatures had been lying in wait in the trees that lined the road and under the very soil of the ground. They surged forward in unstoppable waves. The APCs opened up with their top mounted .50 calibers. Infantry spilled from the transport trucks lobbing grenades into the Kaijus' ranks, their M-16s chattering. The infantry was doing its best to fan out and create a perimeter around the convoy to keep the Kaiju away from it. McCurry rotated his own weapon eastward. Tracer rounds flashed as the general used them to adjust his aim and began hammering at a pack of Kaiju closing in far too fast for his liking.

"Incoming hostiles at four o'clock!" Someone cried out over the com-net.

The warning made no sense to McCurry. The Kaiju were already everywhere. Then he saw them. The Kaiju came sweeping in out of the blue sky on leathery wings. The creatures blotted out the sun above the convoy with their numbers. McCurry knew he and his troops were dead and cursed himself for never considering that the Kaiju might have the cunning to put an ambush like this one together. He shifted his .50 caliber, bringing the weapon's twin barrels upwards. The weapon shook, spitting a continuous stream of fire into the descending Kaiju. The heavy rounds splattered the Kaiju they struck, blowing their frail bodies into a rain of pulp and bone fragments. McCurry recalled reading a report on the winged Kaiju. Unlike their ground based brethren they were weak things with hollow bones, next to no natural armor in comparison, and much smaller brains. Nonetheless, they were deadly. Their speed and just as lethal claws made them a force to be reckoned with.

Only a fraction of the winged Kaiju came directly downward onto the convoy. Most of them concentrated on the attack helicopters that had sped forward to deliver support to the convoy's lead tanks. The helicopters and their crews never stood a chance. The winged Kaiju were on them before they even came about to engage them. The creatures plowed into the helicopters. A few of the winged Kaiju were sliced to bits by the helicopters blades, but even that got their job done. The copters whose blades were struck in such fashion went into out of control spirals, crashing to the earth. The rest of the copters went down as well, though with groups of the winged Kaiju clinging to their main bodies, tearing at them right up until the moment Kaiju and pilots alike died in fiery airborne explosions.

McCurry didn't even bother ordering the convoy into retreat. There was no hope escaping the Kaiju. More and more of the land based Kaiju were coming towards it from as far as the eye could see in every direction. It was like a scene from some zombie movie where the last survivors made their final stand before the screen went black and the credits started to roll.

The huge .50 caliber that McCurry was firing clicked empty, its belt of ammo exhausted. McCurry snatched up the automatic shotgun beside him as several of the winged Kaiju landed on the roof of the APC he rode in. He blew one of the creature's arms clean off its shoulder. The thing shrieked and toppled from the top of the APC. McCurry swept the shotgun around to gut a second one of the winged Kaiju with a near point blank burst. The sounds of weapons' fire was dying out as the cries of the Kaiju grew even louder. McCurry took a final shot that reduced the head of a Kaiju to orange pulp and then ducked inside the APC, slamming the hatch above him closed. He could hear winged Kaiju moving about the vehicle's roof. He also could hear the raging of the ground based Kaiju outside the APC on the road.

Metal screeched and gave way as their claws dug at it. The APC's driver was screaming. McCurry glanced over his shoulder to see the APC's front window had been shattered and a Kaiju was trying to force its body through the opening. The driver was sprawled out in her seat, her throat a red mess of jagged and torn meat.

The side door exploded inward, striking the opposite interior wall. In its wake, Kaiju poured inside. McCurry met them with burst after burst from his automatic shotgun until it too clicked empty. He didn't have a fresh magazine for the automatic shotgun so he tossed it aside, yanking his sidearm from the holster on his hip. He took aim at a Kaiju, holding the pistol in a two handed grip. The Kaiju's head snapped back as he put a round into the thing's forehead. It flopped sideways into another Kaiju, causing it to stumble and go crashing to the APC's floor within reach of McCurry's legs and feet. One of its long arms lashed out. The Kaiju's claws separated McCurry's left leg from his body at his knee. With a pained grunt, McCurry flopped to the floor himself. The impact jarred his weapon from his grasp as the Kaiju that had struck him dragged itself across the floor towards him instead of trying to get to its feet. McCurry kicked at the beast with his right leg. The sole of his combat boot met its nose with a sickening crunch. The blow drove the Kaiju into an even deeper frenzy. It dug both of its clawed hands into the APC's floor and used the strength of its arms to fling itself on top of McCurry.

The general caught the monster and managed to

roll it over using its own momentum against it. It thudded, hard, against the floor beneath him. McCurry hauled back his arm and smashed a fist into its temple. The Kaiju flinched, its eyes burning with pure hatred and anger. McCurry readied himself to strike it again, but froze in place as pain slashed through him. He saw the claws of another Kaiju's hand wriggling in front of him. The hand had pierced him completely and jutted out of his chest. McCurry's body spasmed and jerked as the Kaiju behind him yanked its hand free. Blood flowed from McCurry's mouth, running over his chin in streams of red. His eyes rolled upwards to show only whites as several Kaiju grabbed his collapsing corpse, tearing it apart between them.

****

Mark didn't have a clue how Scott managed it but the grizzled old veteran had gotten the RV's engine going. Scott kicked it into drive.

"Hold on!" Scott yelled as the RV lurched forward. It plowed through rows of tents and it went bouncing across the camp. Scott swerved hard, narrowly avoiding a National Guard jeep that was also on the move amid the chaos of the camp. One of the panicked troops in the jeep sprayed the side of the RV with multiple bursts from his M-16. The passenger side window beside Mark blew out under the onslaught. Danny screamed in pure terror as shards of glass rained over him and Mark. Mark ducked the exploding glass, managing to keep the bulk of it from digging into his skin. He shoved Danny hard to the RV's floor between the driver and passenger's seats. Danny looked at him with wide, frightened eyes.

"It's gonna be okay," Mark said, trying to make himself believe it as he forced out the words.

Mark heard things hitting the exterior of the RV, some of them being dragged under its heavy wheels. *Those sounds aren't people,* he lied to himself, but in truth, he didn't care. All that mattered was getting Danny out of this hell.

Raising his head up again, Mark stared out the shattered window beside him and got his first up close look at a real life Kaiju. The thing was running after the RV. Its lips were smeared with red blood and its claws slashed at empty air in an animal like rage. Mark lifted his shotgun, leaning around in his seat to stick its barrel at the window in the direction of the Kaiju. He squeezed the shotgun's trigger and it bucked in his hands just as the RV ran over some kind of hole or rock. The huge vehicle bounced and Mark's shot went wild, soaring over the Kaiju's head. If the thing even noticed it had been shot at, it didn't care. It kept up its pace in pursuit of the RV.

"Holy mother of…!" Scott wailed.

Mark snapped his head around to see the RV speeding towards the hastily erected fence that ran the length of the camp's perimeter. He reached for Danny as the RV collided with the fence and tore through it. The crash sent Danny flying forward and then rolling back towards the rear of the RV. Mark felt his breath leave his body as he struck the dash. He didn't know what happened to Scott but the RV suddenly veered wildly to the right, and within moments, too quickly for Mark's mind to properly register, flipped over onto its side.

When Mark woke up, the world was dark. At first, he wondered if he had somehow been blinded in the crash before he realized with some relief that night had fallen. His seat belt was the only thing keeping him in place as he hung sideways above the passenger door. His chest was on fire with pain and he tasted his blood in his mouth. Mark knew several of his ribs were broken. Other than that, he had no idea just how badly he was hurt. Regardless of how long he had been out, he still felt as if he was in shock.

Mark's fingers clawed at the seat belt latch, trying to free himself.

"Danny!" he screamed but there was no answer.

Scott's corpse was above him in the driver's seat next to him. There was no question that Scott was dead. His neck was bent at a sharp and unnatural angle. His head dangled limply towards where Mark hung.

"Danny!" Mark screamed again as he finally got the seat belt undone. He dropped onto the passenger door. Mark tried to break his fall with his hands but didn't have the strength to catch his own weight. His hands gave way and his face slammed into the side of the RV. When he lifted his head, fresh blood ran from the nostrils of his nose. Sheer willpower was all that was keeping him conscious as he crawled on his hands and knees into the rear of the RV, hunting for his son.

Danny was nowhere to be found. Mark wasn't sure if that was a good thing or a very bad one.

Finally, he had to rest. He slumped against the RV's wall as the world spun and he struggled not to vomit. After a while, he found the strength to get to his feet. He climbed up and out the opening of the RV's side door area. The door itself was gone. Whether the crash or one of the Kaiju had ripped it from the RV, there was no way to tell for sure in the dim light of the stars.

Several fires burned in the area of the camp behind where the RV rested on its side. Thousands of corpses covered the ground, some of them partially gnawed upon, others left in scattered bits and pieces.

There was no sign of anyone left alive. Thankfully, there was no sign of the Kaiju either.

"Danny!" Mark cried out in the night. No answer came. He wished he had thought to find his shotgun before climbing out of the RV as he sat on top of it, but he wasn't about to risk descending into the large vehicle again. Climbing out of it the first time had cost him enough. It was all he could do to keep moving as it was.

Mark carefully eased himself from the side of the vehicle to the ground. He staggered through the camp searching desperately for any sign of his son. When he came upon the head of an elderly woman, her body nowhere to be seen, he lost it. He fell to his knees, emptying the contents of his stomach onto the grass. Wiping his lips clean with the backside of his hand, he got to his feet again and continued the search for his son long into the night.

Although a gruesome task, looting the dead proved easy once Mark got the stomach for it. By the time the sun rose, he had everything he needed. He had treated his wounds as best as he could with a first aid kit he had dug up in one of the Guardsmen's stations inside the camp. The bandages bound tightly about his wounds helped as did the handfuls of painkillers he popped like candy. He had two pistols holstered on a belt he had removed from a soldier's corpse and carried an M-16. On his back, he carried a pack stuffed with bottled water, what food he could find, and several magazines for his weapons.

He was convinced the Kaiju had moved on out of the area. Otherwise, surely they would have come after him by now. It wasn't exactly like he was trying to keep quiet and maintain a low profile. Every so often, he continued to yell Danny's name in the vain hope that his son would answer him. At one point, before the dawn, he had even shot a signal flare skyward in hopes that his son would see it and come running into his arms.

The only two things Mark did know for sure were that he was alive and his son was out there somewhere. He promised himself he would never stop looking until he found Danny and the two of them were together again.

Scott's RV was far from the only vehicle that had tried to run when the army of lesser Kaiju attacked the refugee camp. Mark hoped someone had found Danny and took the boy with them. The other possibility of what might have happened to his son was one he couldn't allow himself to dwell on. It hurt too much.

Giving the field of bodies one last look through, he staggered westward, leaving the sea of dead behind him.

Epilogue

The President was dead along with most of his staff and congress. He had died during the evacuation of the Pentagon. Admiral Fiore blamed himself. They had waited too long to leave and had paid the price for their arrogance. *Why had they believed they were safe in DC?* He wondered. It was just another place and not even that well of a defended one with so much of the reminder of the military deployed to the west coast and along the Mississippi. The entire eastern part of the United States was lost. Like so much of the rest of the world, it now belonged to the Kaiju.

In good news, the new defensive line along the Mississippi was currently holding, at least for now. It helped that the Navy was able to join the fight there with smaller but well-armed, refitted vessels to reinforce the army and air force efforts there. There were new centers of research being set up in the heartland, under the direction of the leading Kaiju expert, Dr. Johnson. Some of them with engineering slants, others with a biological one, and all geared to coming up with a means to stop the Kaiju once and for all. Admiral Fiore prayed they came up with something to be used effectively against the Kaiju fast. The human race was running out of time.

One of Fiore's aides beside him in the rear of the helicopter that was flying them westward spoke up.

"Sir, I've got new reports coming in from Europe. It appears Britain may not be completely lost."

"Good," Admiral Fiore smiled. "We're going to need all the help we can get if we're going to turn this war around. It's time those monsters learned that the human race is more than just ants to be trampled over."

Author Bio

Eric S Brown is the author of numerous series including the Kaiju Apocalypse series (with Jason Cordova), the Bigfoot War series, the A Pack of Wolves series, the Homeworld series (with Tony Faville and Jason Cordova), the Jack Bunny Bam Bam series, and the Crypto-Squad series (with Jason Brannon). Some of his stand alone books include War of the Worlds plus Blood Guts and Zombies, World War of the Dead, Last Stand in a Dead Land, Into the Light, Sasquatch Lake, and The Weaponer to name only a few. His short fiction has been published hundreds of times throughout both the small press and by larger publishers in markets like the Grantville Gazette and Baen Books' Onward Drake anthology. He has also done the novelizations of films like Boggy Creek: The Legend is True and The Bloody Rage of Bigfoot. The first book of his own Bigfoot War series was released as a feature film from Origin Releasing in September of 2014 and the Walmart Corporation adapted his short story "The Babble Creek Monster" into a short cartoon that was released in October 2014. Eric also writes an ongoing comic book news column for a regional newspaper called The Guide. He lives in North Carolina with his wife and children where he continues to write tales of hungry corpses, giant monsters, and blazing guns. .